sea horse

parrotfish

crown

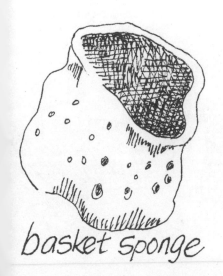

basket sponge

sea star

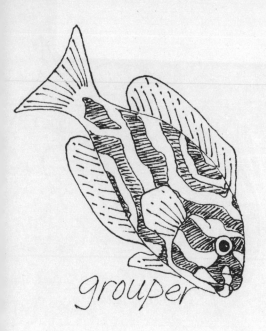

grouper

shark

Jolly Roger

queen angelfish

sea turtle

Pirate
Pink
and
Treasures
of the
REEF

Pirate
Pink
and
Treasures
of the
REEF

Written by Jan Day

Illustrated by Janeen I. Mason

PELICAN PUBLISHING COMPANY
Gretna 2003

With love for Alan and Alicia—J. D.

For Colton, Nathan, and Peyton,
All my love, Nee Nee—J. I. M.

The word "Pelican" and the depiction of a pelican are trademarks
of Pelican Publishing Company, Inc., and are registered
in the U.S. Patent and Trademark Office.

Library of Congress Cataloging-in-Publication Data

Day, Jan, 1943-
  Pirate Pink and treasures of the reef / Jan Day ; illustrated by
Janeen I. Mason.
      p. cm.
Summary: Pink, the daughter of Redbeard, and her first mate Juan battle
pirates and sharks for sunken treasure.
    ISBN 1-58980-086-9 (hard cover : alk. paper)
  [1. Pirates—Fiction. 2. Adventure and adventurers—Fiction. 3. Buried
treasure—Fiction.] I. Mason, Janeen I., ill. II. Title.
  PZ7.D3315 Pi 2003
  [E]—dc21
                                                2002156408

Printed in Korea
Published by Pelican Publishing Company, Inc.
1000 Burmaster Street, Gretna, Louisiana 70053

PIRATE PINK AND TREASURES OF THE REEF

"I'm the daughter of Redbeard, best pirate on the sea. Storm's over. Sun's out. I've treasure to find before the tide comes in."

"Sit down, pirate daughter. Break your toast in bits.
Act like a lady." Her mother sighed and began to stitch.
Pirate manners would never do.

"Ma, I'm the Pirate Pink. I've sailed the high seas. I'll swing from the curtains and slash the cloth."

"You'll do as I say." Ma jumped up and stamped her foot.

In less than a minute Pink slipped out the door.
Ma banged back the shutters till the walls fairly
shook. "Be home before dark," she commanded.

Pink spied her best friend, Juan. "Let's see what the
storm washed in, First Mate," she called.

Juan ran after her down the path to Turtle Bay, past
sea oats hissing in the wind.

"Avast ye!" cried Pink when she saw a ship atilt on the reef. A Jolly Roger rippled from the mizzen.

Juan pulled out his spyglass. "Nobody's home," he
said. Only a seagull ruled what was left of the mast.
"Forward, men," said Pink, swaggering into the waves.

They swam to the bow and hauled themselves over.
Pink shuddered as she climbed aboard the *Barracuda*,
owned by the nasty Captain Snagg.

"Where's the treasure?" Juan shouted. "Didn't they leave me any?" He hopped up and down. "Did they take it all?"

"In the midst of a storm?" Pink said. "I think not."

Juan had not heard of the heartless Snagg, or he would have insisted upon jumping ship.

"I'll take a quick dive," Pink said to Juan, "to see what lies below."

"Me too!" cried Juan. But then he spotted gold coins on the deck. "Aha! I'll keep watch," he said and began stuffing his pockets.

It was growing late. Pink would have to hurry or Ma would be worried. Down she dove into the clear blue water, down as far as her breath would hold.

Wowee, she thought. Treasure chests spilled across the ocean floor. A jeweled bowl, rubies, and coins littered the reef. A queen angelfish watched over her. Its fin shone brighter than any doubloon.

Pink spotted a shy octopus all dolled up with eight strands of pearls. When she saw Pink, she turned red and disappeared in a cloud of ink.

Damselfish shone in the light. *Zounds!* Pink thought. *Their scales are bluer than sapphires on a Spanish crown.*

Pink climbed back on board. "Tomorrow I'll show you treasure, Master Juan, most wondrous to behold."

"I want to see it now," Juan cried, ready to dive in.

"It's time for home!" she shouted. She'd make up to Ma and fry snapper for supper.

But too late they heard the approaching pirate song. "Yo ho ho. We're the meanest men from Cuba to Aruba." Pink and Juan trembled below decks when the loathsome threesome climbed aboard.

"You go down, Mister Billie," the captain commanded, "and put these ropes around them treasure chests. We'll pull 'em up."

"Can't swim, Cap'n. Can't hold me breath."

"Peg Leg Louie, you're my man. There's extra for you and a whipping if you don't."

"No, sir. I'd bob like an apple and never get down."

"Aye rats and barnacles, I'll do it myself."

Just then, young Juan's stomach howled like a hungry whale. It had been a long time since lunch.

"Aye! Thieves on board. Find 'em, men. Tie 'em to the rigging."

Pink leaped out. "My father is the fierce Pirate Redbeard."
Her legs shook like a landlubber's, but she shouted, "If you
hurt us, he'll have you for supper."

"Ha," Captain Snagg cackled. "I'll have you for a snack!"

Pink and Juan tried to dive out of reach, but Snagg scooped them up as if they were the catch of the day.

That was until a shark with a liking for salty old pirates chased after him.

Whew! When it got a whiff of Snagg's stinking stocking feet, the shark gagged and gasped and passed out.

Pink and Juan tumbled down through anemones and seaweed until they caught a ride with a giant turtle going up.

The captain screamed, "Shark! Shark!" as soon as he hit the deck.

The loathsome threesome jumped back in their long-boat and shoved off.

Pink and Juan dove down again to fill the net with gold and jewels and a treasure chest. Then off they rode on the turtle's back.

As Pink waded ashore, she could see Ma there with half the village.

"Where have you been? We've been worried sick," Ma scolded as she kissed her cheek.

Pink gave Ma a big hug. "I really did try to get home before dark."

Juan opened the chest. Everyone gathered 'round. With a scoop of her hand, Pink tossed doubloons into the air. "There's gold for everyone," she said. "It's a gift from the storm."

"I want the gold whistle," said Juan, standing by his pa.
"I want a few coins to buy Pink a proper teatime dress."
Ma smiled. "And, of course, cloth for a brand new sail."
"I want to show you the brightest sea stars on the reef."
Pink took Ma's hand. "And all the treasures underneath."

"Just a quick tour," Ma laughed, and off they sailed
over sizzling silver waves.

sea horse

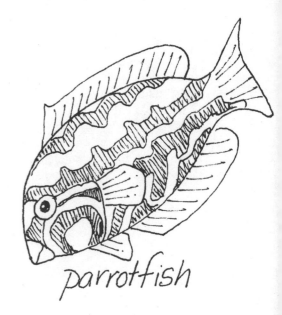

parrotfish

crown

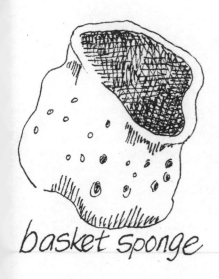

basket sponge

sea star

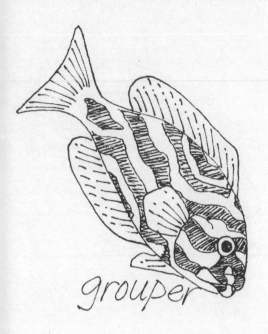

grouper

shark

Jolly Roger

queen angelfish

sea turtle